FOR SAMANTHA, DANIELLA, FRANCESCA AND ALFIE

MILTON
THE AMAZING JUMPING
MOUSE

Story by Tony Orchudesch
Illustrations by Maurice Stevens

MILTON MOUSE

isn't like other mice.

He doesn't run
about very much.

He

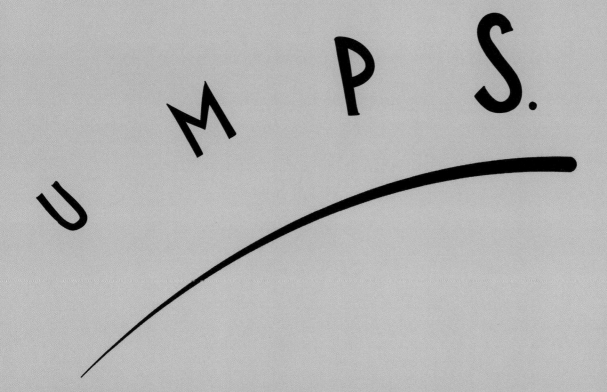

When he was small,
he loved watching the
grasshoppers jumping in the
fields where he lived.

He loved watching
Flip the frog jumping.

He loved watching Chloe the cat jump.

Louie the dog up the road watched too, and Rufus the robin watched everything in

amazement.

Milton wanted
to jump just
like them.

He started to jump
whenever he could.

Milton even jumped
over Bentley the
tortoise.

The tortoise, the frog, the cat, the dog and the robin all became Milton's

friends.

All his friends called him...

Milton the amazing jumping mouse.

REMEMBERING MAURICE

MILION MOUSE

TRAVELS

THE

WORLD

story by Tony Orchudesch

illustrations by Maurice Stevens

Milton Mouse and his friends are
looking at the computer.

They can see the most amazing and

beautiful places.

Strawberry the
magic mouse clicks her ear.

A plane is ready to take off at the airport.

"Where shall we go?" asks Milton.

"Let's go on an adventure!"

"How about Canada? They have beautiful bears there," said Louie the dog.

"That sounds fantastic!" said Milton Mouse. "Let's take a look."

Strawberry clicked her ear again.

The plane took off, whizzing across the sky.
When it landed, the sky was blue and the
sun was hot.

One more click and they were sitting in a small wooden boat, quietly floating down a wide river. They could see huge trees going past them. The trees reached right over the river.

"Look at those huge birds sitting in the trees!" said Rufus the robin.

There were colourful parrots, too.
"Those parrots make a lot of noise!" said Milton.
"Lot of noise!" squawked a parrot. "Lot of noise!"

Milton, Louie and Rufus fell about laughing.
"That's amazing!" said Milton. "I didn't know that
parrots could copy us speaking."
"Copy us speaking!" squawked the parrot.
"COPY US SPEAKING!"

"We could stay here all day," said Milton.
He jumped for joy.
He jumped right over Flip the frog.

The friends climbed back into the boat.

They were all relaxing.

Suddenly, Milton pointed at something.

It was a bright
pink flamingo.

It stood on one leg
and winked at them with one eye.

They decided to stop at a wooden jetty.
Flip the frog was dying to go for a swim. He
dangled his flippers in the cool water.

There was a huge splash and then a

SNAP... !!!

A large, green crocodile leapt out of the water. "Hi there!" said the crocodile. His sharp teeth were very large and there were lots of them.
The crocodile snapped his jaws shut, just missing Rufus the robin.

'Click' went Strawberry the magic mouse.
The colours changed to red and gold.
Now they were in a long canoe
with Louie paddling.

Rufus the robin flew up into the trees.
Forests surrounded them.
They saw a fast-flowing river.

Two large trout leapt out of the water. "They can jump higher than I can!" exclaimed Milton Mouse.

The sky was blue, but the air was cold now.
Milton put on a jumper and a scarf and
jumped out of the canoe.
The water on the lake was calm.
There were high, snowy mountains far away
in the distance.

It was getting late.
"I think it's time to go home,"
said Milton.

Back in the garden, Louie snoozed in his
hammock in the afternoon sun.
Chloe the cat rested next to him.
Flip the frog loved his pond.

"It's nice to be home again," said Rufus.

"Seeing faraway places is great fun, but I do like coming home," said Milton.

For today, the adventure was over...

but Milton Mouse and his friends would go
on lots of other adventures.

AUTHOR

Tony is a music consultant and lives with his family and his piano. When not writing children's stories, he listens to jazz and places songs in commercials on tv and online.

You can contact Tony at www.torchlightmusic.com

Maurice was a graduate in illustration from London's Hornsey School of Art and worked in the US as an art director, before returning to the UK to work as a film and commercials director. He exhibited his watercolours in galleries all over southern England.

ILLUSTRATOR

If you've enjoyed Milton's adventures, please help to spread the word and leave a review on Amazon, Goodreads, Waterstones or any other suitable forum. Each review is hugely appreciated and might just spark a new adventure for Milton.

Printed in Great Britain
by Amazon